slowpoke

slowpoke

Emily Smith Pearce

ILLUSTRATED BY Scot Ritchie

BOYDS MILLS PRESS
Honesdale, Pennsylvania

Text copyright © 2010 by Emily Smith Pearce
Illustrations copyright © 2010 by Scot Ritchie
All rights reserved

Boyds Mills Press, Inc.
815 Church Street
Honesdale, Pennsylvania 18431
Printed in the United States of America

CIP data is available.

First edition
The text of this book is set in 18.5 Century Oldstyle.
The illustrations are done digitally.

10 9 8 7 6 5 4 3 2 1

For Mira, always a quick study

—E.S.P.

To Joanne T., with love

—S.R.

Fiona liked to take her time.

She took her time eating ice cream.

Her ice cream turned to milk.

She took her time in the tub.

Her toes wrinkled.

She took her time feeding the dog.

Her dog fell asleep.

Fiona took her time getting
ready for school.
She brushed each tooth
thirty-two times.
"Hurry up," said her mother.
She changed her clothes
fifty-eight times.

"The bus will leave without you,"
said her father.
She brushed her hair
one hundred strokes.
"You are such a slowpoke,"
said her brother.

Fiona made it to the bus
just in time.

That night her mother ate a plate
of meatloaf in one bite.
Her father watched TV
in fast-forward.
Her brother played Ping-Pong
and the drums
at the same time.
"Why does everyone move so
fast?" asked Fiona.

It all made Fiona's head spin.

The next morning,
Fiona ate her Oaty Loops
one by one.
Her mother yelled,
"The bus is here!"
"Where are my shoes?"
asked Fiona.
The bus pulled away without her.

"Jump in the car, Fiona!"
said her mother.
They drove after the bus.
"I have had it with your
pokiness," said her mother.
"You will start Speed School
next week."

"Not Speed School!" said Fiona.
Her mother boosted her through
the bus door.

Fiona went to Speed School
the next week.

Each student got a pair of goggles.

"The less I see, the faster I will
be," said the teacher. "Say it with
me, class."

Fiona looked at the schedule on the chalkboard.

9:00 a.m. *How to read 500 pages in half an hour*
9:30 a.m. *Cleaning while you sleep*
9:45 a.m. *How to talk, eat, read, jump rope, and add at the same time*

Her head started to spin.

The class had five minutes
for lunch.

"What are you in for?"
asked the kid next to her.

"I missed the bus," said Fiona.

"Me, too," he said.

Fiona started to take a bite.

"Lunch is over!" the lunch lady
yelled. "Line up!"

Fiona's head spun faster.

Fiona ran.

She dashed.

She flew.

She learned to eat like her mom.

She learned to watch TV
like her dad.

She learned to do five things
at once like her brother.

Her head kept spinning.

The next day she sharpened
thirteen pencils at once.
She copied fifty-two sentences
in four minutes.
She packed up her lunch box,
folder, notebook,
and erasers in less than
one second.
A class record!
Her parents clapped and cheered.
She was finished with
Speed School.

Now Fiona could eat
an ice-cream cone
before you could say
"lickety-split."
"Wonderful," said her mother.
She could shower in five
seconds flat.
"Good job," said her father.

She could wash dishes, brush
her teeth, and clean her room
at the same time.

"Guess they taught you
something," said her brother.
Fiona's head was spinning too
fast to answer.

But Fiona could not taste her
ice cream.
She could not enjoy a soak
in the tub.
The dishes, her teeth, and her
room never seemed clean.
She had a very bad crick
in her neck.

One day, Fiona was eating doughnuts, listening to music, painting a picture, and dribbling a basketball at the same time. Her head spun around so fast it stuck.
Backward.

She took off her goggles.

"Help!" she called.

Her mother came running.

Her father dashed to her side.

Her brother skated in.

"I can't go so fast anymore!"

said Fiona.

"But you were doing so well,"
said her mother.
"You were always on time,"
said her father.

"Let's make a deal," said Fiona.
"I will be on time for the bus if
you all go to my Slow School."
"Why would we want to go
slow?" said her brother.
"Wait and see," said Fiona.

Slow School began the next day.

Fiona handed everyone a big pair

of glasses.

"Say it with me: the more I see,

the better my day will be."

She gave them a class schedule.

"Now, rip it up!" she said.

"But—," said her mother.

"Take off your watches, too,"

said Fiona.

Fiona took her family on a walk
down the street.

"I never saw those flowers
before," said her mother.

Next they climbed a tree.

"This is fun," said her brother.

They ate supper one bite at a time.

"This is so tasty!" said her father.

Fiona smiled. It was the same

old meatloaf.

At the end of the day, Fiona's
head began to unstick.

"We should do this more often,"
said her father.

"The flowers *were* pretty,"
said her mother.

"Slow doesn't stink," said her
brother, "if you're not waiting
for the bathroom."

That reminded Fiona.

She left to run a hot bath.

She sat in the tub until

her toes wrinkled.

Her head did not spin at all.

The next day, Fiona's family went
back to their fast ways.
Fiona went back to taking
her time.

But sometimes her father
ate slowly.
Sometimes her mother
planted flowers.
Sometimes her brother did only
one thing at a time.

Fiona caught the bus—
most of the time.

And when the family took
a walk together,
they always took their time.